09/05/1995

CM: I know you're just trying to help, but you need to be careful. Addison, do you hear me? Please be careful when you step on and off the stool. Okay?

AM: Okay.

CM: Thank you.

AM: Is that how Grandpa fell?

CM: Here, hand me that bowl. Now give me the towel. See how I wipe the entire thing down—the bottom, the edges? We can't put wet dishes in Grandma's cupboards. Remember? Here, you try. That's better.

AM: Mommy?

CM: Yes, Addison?

AM: Did you want Grandpa to die?

CM: What? No. Nobody wanted Grandpa to die. You hear me? Nobody.

AM: Then why did Grandpa die?

CM: We all die eventually, sweet pea. Some people get sick. Some people die from accidents. Some die just from old age.

AM: Why?

CM: Because we can't live forever.

AM: Why can't we live forever?

CM: Because we just can't. It's not how it works; it's not how we work. That hasn't stopped people from trying, though.

AM: What do you mean?

CM: People have been trying to figure out how to live forever for years. They build things, they tinker with new medicines—

AM: Tinker?

CM: It means to play with. To explore.

AM: Explore?

CM: Yeah, sweetie, explore.

AM: What do they explore?

CM: Lots of things. Diets, exercise, pills, treatments.

AM: But they haven't figured out how to live forever yet?

CM: Addison, come on, what did I just say a minute ago?

AM: Be careful stepping on the stool.

CM: Yes. Thank you. But not yet, no, people haven't figured it out. Maybe when you're all grown up they'll have it so you can just eat a piece of chocolate and live forever.

AM: I'd like that.

CM: You would, would you?

AM: Yeah. I don't like death.

CM: What don't you like about it, sweetie?

AM: It's scary.

CM: It is. I know it is. Do you wish that Grandpa could've lived forever?

AM: Yeah.

CM: I understand.

AM: I wish he wouldn't have died because then Grandma wouldn't have made me cry.

CM: How did Grandma make you cry?

AM: She cried in the church, and she wouldn't stop crying, and I cried at her crying.

CM: It's never easy to see those we love in tears.

AM: I love Grandma.

CM: I do too, sweet pea.

AM: Did you love Grandpa?

CM: Here, just set that heavy dish on the table. We'll take care of that one later.

AM: Mommy?

CM: Yes, honey?

AM: Did you love Grandpa?

CM: There were times that—well, did you love him?

AM: I didn't like it when he was mean to Grandma.

CM: He wasn't very nice to your daddy either.

AM: His voice was scary when he yelled.

CM: Yes, it was. We all yell, though. Daddy yells. I yell. Even you yell.

AM: I yell?

CM: Of course you yell, silly.

AM: Wyatt yells.

CM: Wyatt yells pretty loud, doesn't he?

AM: Mmhm.

CM: And you love Wyatt, right?

AM: Yes. I love Wyatt very much.

CM: I know you do. And that's what I think I'm trying to get at somehow. People do things that make us sad, that make us mad, they say things they don't mean, but we—well, we just keep on loving them, don't we?

AM: Does Daddy make you mad?

CM: Your daddy makes me mad all the time.

AM: All the time?

CM: All the time.

AM: But you still love him, no matter what?

CM: No matter what. I mean, how many times a day do you see me kiss your daddy?

AM: Once in the morning, once before bed, and as many times as you can between.

CM: And can you remember why do we do that, Addison?

AM: I don't remember.

CM: Oh come on, yes you do. In the hospital, before Grandpa went to sleep, what did Grandma say to you? When she sat you on her lap, what did she say?

AM: Kisses con—kisses con—.

CM: Kisses conquer all. That's right. They help us forget the yelling. They help us forget the crying. Grandma says it all the time: kisses conquer all. And now she said that to you, didn't she?

AM: Yeah.

CM: Listen, sweet pea: we kiss those we love as often as we can because we just don't know how much longer we have with them. Do you understand?

AM: I understand.

CM: Good. Good, good.

01/18/2000

CM: Mrs. Price—

KP: Ms. Price.

CM: Ms. Price, I don't think we're quite understanding you. Is she kissing her desk? Her book? Her locker? A plunger? What?

KP: No, Mrs. Myers. I'm afraid Addison has been kissing each and every boy and girl in her class. She gives out kisses while the students are hanging their coats. She gives out kisses during recess, as well as at the end of the day, before the students walk to their buses. She has even tried giving kisses out to Mr. Borming, while he has attempted to diffuse the situation time and time again.

CM: Jesus.

KP: As you can imagine, there have been some complaints. Parents have called Principal Eaves and have begun to question the ways in which the school is run.

HM: Which parents?

KP: That isn't relevant, Mr. Myers.

HM: I think wanting to know who has a problem with my daughter is relevant.

KP: Let me rephrase, then: I can't give out that information. Even if I could, I wouldn't. Because the other parents and their phone calls are not the issue here.

HM: But my daughter is an issue?

KP: I'm not saying Addison is an issue, sir. But her behavior most definitely is.

CM: Has she said anything? I mean, does she say anything about why she's kissing?

KP: She has. But sense has yet to be entirely made from her responses. Which is why you're here—details need to be gleaned; gaps need to be filled. Mr. Borming, who has witnessed this issue first hand, and who has asked Addison on multiple occasions about her behavior, believes that Addison is a frightened child.

HM: Frightened? Of what?

KP: That she's going to lose her classmates, Mr. Myers. When Mr. Borming has asked her why she feels the need to kiss her classmates, she has replied on multiple occasions with something along the lines of not knowing if she'll see any of them tomorrow. Has she said anything of the sort to either of you at home?

HM: No—

CM: Yes—

HM: When? When has she said something like that?

CM: I don't know. But she has, Hud. To me. To Wyatt.

HM: Well, I've never heard it.

KP: And you didn't see that as a problem, Mrs. Myers?

HM: She's ten years old. Kids her age say things they don't mean all the time.

CM: How long has this been going on, Ms. Price?

KP: It's been happening for about seven weeks now.

CM: Seven weeks?

KP: Maybe even longer. The first reported incident occurred sometime during the second week of December. While you wouldn't be wrong in wanting either myself or my colleagues to contact you immediately, Mr. Myers is right in saying that overreaction isn't the best approach. That said, we'd decided to let it play out, acting under the assumption that what had occurred, and what continued to occur, was a phase, perhaps even a product of the Y2K scare. We thought maybe she was just acting out of fear, that, coupled with what she explained her reasoning to be, she'd simply seen too much on the news. But, as you know, Y2K came and went. The kissing continued. Here we are.

CM: Okay. Okay. Okay, so what comes next? What do we do? She gets to stay in school, doesn't she?

KP: In no way do we intend to remove Addison from school. Please don't worry about that. All we'd like you to do today is answer a few questions. From there, we all can decide how best to go about this.

HM: Now just wait a minute. I understand what you're saying. Really, I do. I understand how this can be viewed as an issue. But, do you honestly think our daughter—that girl out in the hall, slumped against a locker, thinking she's started the apocalypse—is doing something so wrong here? Maybe I'm missing something, but is kissing really that bad? Would you rather have her sit at her desk and do nothing? Say nothing? Feel nothing?

KP: Try and think of this from my point of view, Mr. Myers, from another parent's point of view. Imagine your daughter being ill—carrying something contagious—and continuing this behavior. I can only assume you've heard of mononucleosis. Meningitis? Imagine several children contracting that illness. Are we to shut the school down then, because of a kiss? Spread of illness is only the first tier of this issue. I mean, if something of that magnitude were to happen, it isn't like Addison would be the one and only culprit. It's a school. Illness walks in and out of here every day. The second tier of this issue, however, the one I'd be most concerned about, is what would happen if we were to let this just run its course without interruption. A year goes by: she's still kissing boys and girls. Fine. But three years from now, four years from now, once she's menstruating, what then? Beyond the cruelty of the words she'd hear, what if the kissing advanced to other activities, with several partners? You're talking about sexually transmitted diseases, you're talking about pregnancy…I have plenty of statistics to offer, if that'll help support what I'm saying to you.

HM: No thanks, Ms. Price, you've said enough. And you've wasted enough of my time. I'll see you at home, Caroline.

CM: Hud, where are you going?

HM: Plenty of streets that need plowing before dark, don't you think?

— :

CM: I'm sorry about that, Ms. Price.

KP: It's quite all right, Caroline. Can I call you that?

CM: Of course.

KP: If you'd prefer, we can hold off on the questions until the next time your husband is present. Or, we can proceed as outlined. I promise, the questions won't take much of your time.

CM: Sure. Sure, we can go ahead. I'll just catch him up later. I'm really sorry he acted like that though. Truly.

KP: It's okay, Caroline. It's normal for strong feelings to arise from protector types; they feel threatened by the issue with their child; they feel like they've failed. But, let's get started. My first question is: Has there been a death in the family recently?

CM: Not recently. No, the most recent one was five years—yeah, about five years ago now—Hudson's father died.

KP: I'm sorry to hear that. How'd he go?

CM: He'd had a long battle with prostate cancer.

KP: Was Addison close with him?

CM: I wouldn't say she was close, no. She saw him, sure, she knew most of what was going on. But close? No, I wouldn't say that.

KP: What about Wyatt?

CM: He was closer to him than Addison was, definitely.

KP: And what kind of a relationship do Wyatt and Addison share?

03/03/2003

WM: She's being a little slut.

CM: Watch your mouth!

WM: Those aren't 'my' words.

HM: Then why the hell would you say them? Think that's any way to talk about your sister?

WM: You don't see her every day, Dad, not like I do.

HM: You're right. I don't. But if I did, I can promise you I wouldn't call her a slut. Look what you did to your mother.

CM: I'm fine.

WM: Mom, I didn't mean it. Really. It's just, well, didn't we get this taken care of?

HM: Told you therapy wasn't worth a damn.

CM: Dr. Monaghan says that she's improving, that she's starting to open up.

WM: I'm not trying to be insensitive, but I don't think I'd call her taking random dudes into bathrooms and kissing them an improvement.

HM: At least it's just dudes now. That's a plus, isn't it, having that part figured out?

CM: Hud, stop it.

HM: What? I find that to be a relief, Caroline.

WM: I'd rather they be girls, honestly. There'd be a lot less bragging and high-fiving.

CM: Stop. It doesn't matter what you'd prefer. It doesn't matter what either of you would prefer. Wyatt, be honest— she just chooses random boys and drags them into the bathroom? You've seen that happen?

WM: I haven't seen it, no. But I hear it, Mom. I hear all about it. If I don't hear it from Rick or Jordy, it's from some freshman whose friend just cut class and walked over to the middle school.

HM: Wait, Rick and Jordy are—

WM: Jesus, Dad, no. They hear things and pass them on to me. Listen to what I'm saying. Please?

CM: So they're approaching her now?

WM: The freshmen? Why wouldn't they? Freshmen are desperate.

HM: I'd say. To walk that far—

CM: Dammit Hudson, I'd really appreciate it if you took this seriously. It's not something to be blown off.

HM: You want me to be serious?

CM: I think that now would be a better time than any to be serious.

HM: Fine. I'll be serious. Wyatt, you know who these guys are, right?

WM: Most of them.

HM: Then beat the shit out of them. They talk about her like that? Punch them in the nose. They make that walk to the middle school? You leave class straight away and punch them in the nose.

CM: You're unbelievable.

HM: You asked for serious. This is as serious as I get.

WM: You really think that's going to help, Dad?

HM: I do, yes. Addison's reputation isn't going to change, so you change the narrative with your action. Word gets around that those in pursuit of Addison have an obstacle, they'll slow their pursuit.

CM: What about the discipline that's sure to come from that? Wyatt turns into the enforcer, patrols the schools with his fists. Addison slows down, but Wyatt doesn't go to college—because Wyatt goes to jail, because Wyatt's tethered to the house. Meanwhile, Addison's alone at school, and we're worse than we were at square one.

HM: I'm not saying Wyatt keeps the act up day after day. I'm saying that he punches a couple of them, off school grounds, preferably, and it's going to make a big difference.

WM: I'm not punching anyone, Dad.

CM: I'm all ears for whenever you have another 'serious' suggestion.

WM: But what about me?

HM: What about you?

WM: I'm tired of hearing about this shit.

CM: Language.

WM: Every day, I get made fun of for her being my sister. Every day, some new smiling jackass walks up to me and says how he can't wait to bone Addison.

HM: They say things like that?

WM: Yes. They do.

HM: What are their names?

WM: Their names don't matter, Dad.

HM: Why am I the only one that thinks it matters that someone tells them they can't say that about someone? Why am I the only one who thinks bad behavior should be corrected by those that have the means to correct it?

CM: Because it isn't that simple, Hud. There are repercussions to everything.

WM: I'm still not hearing any suggestions on what I should do.

CM: What about me?

WM: Huh?

CM: What about me, Wyatt? You don't think I deal with parents all day? You don't think that they come into Mandrell's and look at me like I'm telling Addison to do all of this? That I'm behind all of this? Of course they don't say anything about it. No, they keep it professional, ask me to explain their current policy, inquire about the next step. But they know exactly who I am. They know who my daughter is.

HM: You know that extension of the courthouse we're helping build? People have been driving by, and walking by, and they've been waving, but they stare, too. Make sure it's who they think it is. Lean over to their kid or spouse and tell them whose father I am. Walking into the courthouse itself is worse. Much worse. All that small talk, always tiptoeing. I hate it. Every second of it.

WM: So we're obviously all affected by this. What do we do then? Home school?

CM: And have me or your father quit our jobs? We can't afford that.

HM: What if we send her away?

CM: Send her where?

HM: I don't know. Idaho, Colorado.

CM: Boarding school?

HM: Why not?

CM: I don't think opting out of the problem and forcing someone else to solve it is the best route.

WM: Isn't that essentially what you're doing with her therapy?

CM: Look, I just don't think a different zip code would solve the problem.

HM: Well, what else is there?

WM: Lock her in her room. Tell her she's Sleeping Beauty or something.

CM: Brilliant plan, Wyatt.

WM: I don't hear you suggesting anything.

CM: What if we just stay the course? Have her keep going to therapy, let that do its thing. Deal with the comments, the looks. We stay patient, we lean on one another, we stay—
AM: I'll stop.

— :

HM: Hey sweetheart.
WM: How long have you been listening?
AM: I said I'd stop, didn't I? I do what you want. Isn't that how this is supposed to work?
CM: Sweet pea, you don't—sweet pea, don't cry, come here.

11/10/2004

QR: Little cold for a walk, isn't it?
AM: What?
QR: I said, it's a little cold for a walk, isn't it?
AM: I'm fine.
QR: Tell that to your cheeks and nose.

— :

QR: I'm Quentin, by the way.
AM: I know who you are.
QR: Come on, hop in.

AM: I'm fine, thanks.

QR: Your brother would kick my ass if I just drove off.

AM: He should kick his own ass then.

QR: He left you here?

— :

QR: Why?

AM: Such a mystery.

QR: Come on, I'll take you home. Either I take you home, or I drive alongside you the whole way.

AM: Prepare yourself for a slow go of it then.

QR: At least let me cut a couple miles off for you. Call it hitchhiking. I need to stop for gas anyway.

AM: Should I stick out my thumb to make it more real?

QR: If it'll make you feel better.

— :

AM: It smells like feet in here.

QR: Sorry. Conditioning started Monday.

AM: Wyatt wanted to try out this year.

QR: Why didn't he?

AM: Could be that he sucks at basketball. Could be that my dad told him to get a job. Could have something to do with me. I don't know. Never said.

QR: Oh.

AM: Yeah. Oh.

QR: Did I say something wrong?

AM: Wrong? No. Oh's just the worst possible thing to say.

QR: Okay. No more, 'oh'. Does that mean tonight you—

AM: Go ahead.

QR: Go ahead what?

AM: Ask me who. That's everyone's first question: who? As if that's all that matters, who-who-who.

QR: Look around. We live in a town of, what, 2,000 people? What you do, and who you do it with, it's going to be talked about. 'Who' does matter. To some, it really is all that matters.

AM: That's why I can't wait to get out of this damn place.

QR: You're thirteen years old.

AM: Fourteen.

QR: Okay, fourteen.

AM: And that means I can't want something?

QR: That isn't what I said. Look, you wanting to get out of here is normal. I do too. But I'm seventeen. I'm gone before summer hits.

AM: So?

QR: What I'm saying is that you should probably try as hard as you can to get that thought out of your head. The next couple of years are going to eat you up if you don't.

AM: Where are you heading off to?

QR: Oregon. Salem, Oregon.

AM: What college?

QR: To hell with college. Overpriced. Worthless to me. My dad lives in Salem. He's one of those guides for when you want to go hiking, or kayaking, or whatever.

AM: Is that what you want to do, you know, for your job?

QR: Maybe. I don't know. I'm trying to manage expectations, but I thought I'd at least get a taste and see what I think. My dad said falling into it was one of the best things that happened to him. I have to get out and pump; you staying here?

AM: I'll get out.

—:

QR: Does Wyatt know what he's going to do yet, when he's done?

AM: He wouldn't tell me if he knew.

QR: I sit near him in chemistry. All he does is doodle. Thought maybe he was hoping for an art school or something.

AM: What does my asshole brother doodle?

QR: Just shapes, I think.

AM: Oh.

QR: Pretty quiet kid.

AM: Didn't used to be that way.

QR: What happened?

AM: Me.

— *:*

QR: If you were so accepting of it all, if you believed in what you were doing, I don't think you'd be so down on yourself. So why do it then? Is it some kind of disease?

AM: A disease?

QR: Disease, condition, whatever.

AM: I don't think so. I don't know. Maybe. But it's what people expect of me now. Guys just come to me, won't take no for an answer, not from the girl that made out with Carl Treehorn, or the girl that gave Vance Barnes a handjob. 'What do those douche bags have that I don't?' they say, 'Why them and not me?' So, I make them happy. Because isn't that what you're supposed to do? Do things to make others happy? Isn't that what we're told our purpose is?

QR: You really gave Barnes a handjob?

AM: Yeah. Why?

QR: Barnes?

AM: Yes, fucking Barnes. So what? You want me to tell you how big of a dick he has? You want to know how fast he blew it?

QR: No, no. I'm just surprised is all.

AM: At what?

QR: Most girls aren't so open about something like that.

AM: Yeah, well.

QR: Going inside to pay. You thirsty or anything?

AM: I'm fine.

QR: Okay. But I think you're wrong.

AM: About what?

QR: I don't think making others happy should come at the expense of yourself, or others, for that matter.

AM: It always does, though. Make one person happy, you make another sad. By hurting someone, you help someone else. Give and take.

QR: Whatever you say. You sure you don't want anything?

AM: I'm fine.

— :

QR: Can't beat two for two bucks. Which one do you want?

AM: Dr. Pepper.

QR: You still live on South Thompson?

AM: Yeah.

QR: Want me to drop you off somewhere nearby? Let you walk the rest of the way, show Wyatt how tough you are?

AM: I don't need to prove anything.

QR: Front door it is.

AM: Quentin?

QR: What?

22

AM: How many girls have you kissed?

QR: How many?

AM: Yeah. How many?

QR: Why do you want to know?

AM: Maybe I want to know how weird I really am. Or maybe it's that I want to feel normal. Tell me.

QR: One.

AM: One?

QR: Yeah, one.

AM: Just one?

QR: Yeah, just one. Is there a problem with that? How weird does that make you feel? Does that make you feel normal? Jesus.

AM: I feel no different.

QR: Well?

AM: Well what?

QR: Aren't you even going to ask who it was?

AM: I told you, the who doesn't matter.

QR: It does to me. The who is supposed to mean something.

AM: Who was it then?

QR: Chelsea Geist.

AM: She's pretty. Like, model pretty.

QR: She is.

AM: Did you like her?

QR: I loved her. That's why I kissed her.

AM: Do you still love her?

QR: Some days I do. Other days not so much.

AM: When she's dangling herself over Brent?

QR: Yeah.

AM: They're inseparable.

QR: I know.

AM: But let's back up a bit. If I kissed you right now, would it mean that I love you?

QR: What? That's not what I said. That's not what I said at all.

AM: Yes, it is. You just said that love drives a kiss. So why can't a kiss drive love? Can't kissing make people feel loved to the point that it can make an awful day stop on a dime?

QR: That's quite a thought for someone your age.

AM: Years of being fed over and over what people are 'supposed' to do has a way of making you think for yourself. Just answer my question, Quentin.

QR: Which one?

AM: Can't kissing make people feel loved?

QR: I guess, yeah, but—

AM: But what? You can't just go around kissing strangers? Yeah, I've heard. But why not? Ask anyone I've ever kissed, they'll remember that day. Surprised? Sure, some were. But angry? Disappointed? Not for a second.

QR: I think that you'd feel differently if you'd ever been in love. You'd know that a kiss has more value than you're giving it now. That it's more sacred. You'd know that a kiss is a reflection of that feeling and it happens because the moment has been built up to the point that you don't know what else to say, that you don't know what else to do with your hands, or your eyes or your lips.

— :

QR: Have you ever felt that?

— :

QR: That's it ahead, right?

AM: Yeah. Yellow mailbox. Here's fine though.

QR: Here you are, Addison.

AM: I would say thank you, but I didn't ask for any of this.

— :

QR: Aren't you going to get out?

AM: I don't want to.

QR: What do you want to do then?

AM: Talk. I want to keep talking with you about love.

11/19/2004

DA: Mrs. Myers, I'm Detective Andrews and this is Detective Trestman, how are you this afternoon?

CM: Hello.

DA: We came here today to share some new information on the whereabouts of your daughter, a Ms. Addison Myers. Can we come in?

CM: Sure, sure. Of course. Have a seat.

DT: You have a very lovely home, Mrs. Myers.

CM: Thank you, Detective—Trestman, was it?

DT: That's right, ma'am.

CM: Would either of you like some coffee? I just made a pot. Or juice?

DA: Coffee, please. Black will be just fine.

DT: Same here. Thank you, ma'am.

DA: I understand you're the only one home today, Mrs. Myers.

CM: Yes, it's just me. My husband and my son stepped out for a bit.

DT: Do you have any idea as to where they went?

CM: They didn't say. They just said they were heading out.

— :

DA: Mmm, now that's some good coffee.

26

DT: Yes, very good. Thank you, ma'am.

CM: You said you have some new information on Addison?

DA: We do. But first, I wanted to let you know that, as we speak, Hudson and Wyatt are being escorted back to the house here.

CM: Escorted?

DT: Yes ma'am. It's more of a precaution than anything else.

DA: I'm sure Officer Thomas informed you that, since the night of Addison's disappearance, we've had eyes on your house for any unusual activity. So, naturally, when Hudson and Wyatt loaded shotguns into separate vehicles and took off at the exact same time, we had patrol cars ready to tail.

DT: While we understand the frustration all of you must feel, it wouldn't be helpful for our investigation if they were to take the law into their own hands.

CM: I understand.

DT: To let you know, in case he brings it home with him, your husband wasn't especially happy about our apprehension of he and Wyatt. But Wyatt understood right away.

DA: He seems like a good kid.

CM: He is.

DT: He was supposed to bring Addison home from school that day, wasn't he?

CM: Yes. Yes, he was.

DA: And he didn't because he was upset with her?

CM: Yes, that's correct. He feels horrible about it now b—

DA: Guilt's quite a natural thing in this scenario, Mrs. Myers. It's likely to subside after we find Addison, though.

DT: And we will find her. We're all working very hard on that. These things happen more often than you'd think, ma'am, which means we're all the more capable of getting your daughter back, and quickly.

CM: Officer Thomas mentioned that. Technology, he said, leaps and bounds.

DA: That's correct. And it's served us well so far in your daughter's case.

CM: What do you mean?

DT: Ma'am, what do you know about Quentin Reede?

CM: Quentin Reede? The name sounds familiar. I want to say that he's in Wyatt's class but I'm not sure.

DA: Yes, yes he is.

CM: What about him? Do you think he's the one that took her?

DT: We've been led to believe that, yes, your daughter is with Mr. Reede.

DA: We've had an Officer Barrow maintain a close eye on the attendance records at Bottineau High School and, it turns out, Mr. Reede is the only student other than Addison who has been absent each school day since her disappearance.

DT: All seven of 'em.

DA: Which is a substantial amount, especially when, after questioning his mother—a Gabrielle Tedesky, remarried—we discovered that not only had Quentin not been showing any signs of illness, she, more importantly, hadn't seen him for over a week.

DT: We asked her whether or not she found that odd—odd enough to notify someone—to which she replied more or less that she just thought he'd been staying with a friend.

DA: Her ignorance, while perplexing, didn't appear to be an attempt to cover anything up.

CM: So Addison's with Quentin?

DT: We can't say that with absolute certainty, at least not yet.

DA: But it is a lead, a strong lead, which is more than we've had so far.

CM: But why? What the hell would Quentin Reede want with my daughter?

DT: Well, ma'am, you said it yourself that your daughter was a bit, uh, how do I say it, promiscuous

CM: Yes. I don't know if that's the word I used, but—

DA: It's only a matter of time before a predator pounces on that type of behavior, Mrs. Myers.

CM: Does Quentin have a record of doing that? Are we talking about sexual assault here?

DT: No, ma'am. I mean, we can't rule such a thing out but, as for Quentin's record, it's clean. One speeding ticket, one parking ticket.

DA: Which understandably makes all of this a bit foggier than one would expect, as there doesn't seem to be a clear motive.

DT: For all we know, Addison asked him to take her.

DA: It isn't a stretch of the imagination to say so, considering her past.

DT: What Detective Trestman actually means is that kids do these things, ma'am. Sometimes without reason. Or, if there is reason, of any sort, they can't even put it into words. The important thing, though, is that we get her back here.

CM: When do you think that will be?

DA: Sooner rather than later, Mrs. Myers.

DT: Mrs. Tedesky was rather helpful in telling us that a few months back Quentin's father gave Quentin a credit card of his to use, you know, in case of emergency. We've been tracing that card.

DA: The last purchase made here in Bottineau was at the Shell station downtown. Gasoline, one Dr. Pepper and one Diet Pepsi. The next purchase made with the credit card was at a Wal-Mart in Williston. Two pillows, two blankets. Then, breakfast at Denny's in Miles City, Montana. A few more minor things after that—

DT: The last stop we have on record is in Bend, Oregon. Gasoline.

CM: Oregon?

DA: The boy's father lives in Salem. We believe that's where they're headed.

DT: Do you have any family in Oregon? Any friends? Any reason for Addison to go along with this?

CM: No. I've never even been to Oregon.

DA: Has Hudson?

CM: No, not that I know of.

DT: What about Wyatt?

CM: No. Never. Salem, Oregon?

DT: Yes ma'am.

CM: Is that where they're going to be taken into custody?

DA: In addition to calling the boy's father, we've alerted the Salem Police Department, as well as every other law enforcement agency in that area. We've faxed them photographs, statements, what have you.

DT: Needless to say, that's where we anticipate they'll be apprehended. From there, they'll be transported back to Bottineau and we'll proceed accordingly.

CM: Quentin Reede? Salem, Oregon?

DT: I know this is probably a lot to take in. I mean, we know how rough this can be on a mother as caring as you. Just try to stay as positive as you can, and please do call us if you need anything, anything at all. Okay?

CM: Okay. I'll do that, Detective Trestman.

DA: You ready there, Paul?

DT: Thank you very much for the coffee, ma'am.

CM: No, thank you. You don't know how much of a relief this is, to actually have an idea.

DT: There will certainly be more to come, ma'am. Take care now.

CM: Wait. Detectives?

DA: Yes, Mrs. Myers?

CM: Once they're taken into custody, can you please give me a call? I'd just like to know all that I can before I see my daughter.

DA: Of course. What we hear, you'll hear.

Q&A

a *Strays Like Us* story by Garrett Francis

ABOUT THE AUTHOR

Garrett Francis is the author of the novel *And in the Dark They Are Born* and the short story collection *Strays Like Us*. He grew up on a small farm in Michigan and earned his B.A. in Creative Writing from Grand Valley State University.

In 2012, Garrett co-founded *Squalorly*, a digital literary journal of the Midwest and served as its nonfiction editor until 2014.

In 2016, founded Orson's Publishing in 2016, a micro press and served as the press's sole editor (and designer, and publicist, among other roles) until its closure in 2020, publishing four book-length works by new and emerging authors.

He also founded *Orson's Review* in 2017, a digital literary journal that served as a companion to its parent press, publishing fiction, creative nonfiction, poetry and photography. He served as the sole editor of *Orson's Review* as well, and is proud to have helped bring the work of over 70 international contributors to life.

Today, Garrett lives in the Pacific Northwest with his family. Short works of his have been published in literary journals like *Midwestern Gothic*, *Barely South Review*, *Whiskeypaper* and *Monkeybicycle*.

###

Visit authorgarrettfrancis.com to learn more about Garrett and his work.

Copyright © Garrett Francis, 2024.

All rights reserved. No parts of this book may be copied, distributed, or published in any form without permission from the publisher. For permissions contact: authorgarrettfrancis@gmail.com

This is a work of fiction in which all events and characters in this book are completely imaginary. Any resemblance to actual people is entirely coincidental.

ISBN: 978-1-7338171-7-2

Published by 5626 Press